D0607638

TO MY SISTERS, NEL, JEN, FAY, AND VAL,
WHO COOK JUST LIKE MOM
—G.A.

TO GRANDMA THELMA, GRANDMA STEPHANIE,
GRANDDADDY JAMES, AND GRANDDADDY D—
THANK YOU FOR POURING SO MUCH INTO ME.
—S.W.

Text copyright © 2022 by Glenda Armand
Jacket art and interior illustrations copyright © 2022 by Steffi Walthall
All rights reserved. Published in the United States by Crown Books for Young Readers,
an imprint of Random House Children's Books, a division of Penguin Random House LLC, New York.
Crown and the colophon are registered trademarks of Penguin Random House LLC.

Visit us on the Web! rhcbooks.com
Educators and librarians, for a variety of teaching tools, visit us at RHTeachersLibrarians.com

Library of Congress Cataloging-in-Publication Data
Names: Armand, Glenda, author. | Walthall, Steffi, illustrator.
Title: Black-eyed peas and hoghead cheese : a story of food, family, and freedom /
by Glenda Armand ; illustrated by Steffi Walthall.
Description: First edition. | New York : Crown Books for Young Readers, [2022] |
Includes bibliographical references. | Audience: Ages 3–7. | Audience: Grades K–1. |
Summary: As Frances helps her grandmother with New Year's Day dinner, Grandma teaches her the origins
of the different dishes and soul food they prepare together. Includes a recipe for Fay's Fabulous Pralines.
Identifiers: LCCN 2021056961 | ISBN 978-0-593-48614-6 (hardcover) |
ISBN 978-0-593-48615-3 (library binding) | ISBN 978-0-593-48616-0 (ebook)
Subjects: CYAC: Cooking—Fiction. | Grandmothers—Fiction. | African Americans—Fiction. |
LCGFT: Picture books. Classification: LCC PZ7.A697 Bl 2022 | DDC [E]—dc23

MANUFACTURED IN CHINA   10 9 8 7 6 5 4 3 2 1   First Edition

BLACK-EYED PEAS
AND HOGHEAD CHEESE

A STORY OF FOOD, FAMILY, AND FREEDOM

BY
GLENDA ARMAND

ILLUSTRATED BY
STEFFI WALTHALL

♛

CROWN BOOKS FOR YOUNG READERS
NEW YORK

Mmmm. I close my eyes and follow the sweet potato pies with my nose as Grandma moves them from the oven to the windowsill.

There's no place I'd rather be than right here in Grandma's kitchen.

Mom, Dad, and I came all the way from California to spend the holidays with our family. Soon it will be New Year's Day, and everyone will be here.

Mom and Dad are staying with Auntie Betty. So today I have Grandma all to myself.

I put on my apron, and I'm ready to help her prepare the New Year's Day dinner.

Know what I like most about Grandma's kitchen?

More than jambalaya? More than sweet potato pie? Even more than pralines?

Grandma's stories! Every meal Grandma cooks comes with a story.

What will today's story be?

"Time for black-eyed peas, *Tifi*," Grandma says.

Tifi sounds like "tee-FEE," and it means "little girl" in Creole. That's Grandma's first language.

Grandma spreads the black-eyed peas on a towel.

My job is to pluck out any tiny stones or broken peas.

"We can't celebrate the New Year without black-eyed peas," Grandma says.

I can tell that a story is about to begin as I find a pebble. "Why, Grandma?"

"Well, Frances"—Grandma calls me by my name this time—"many years ago, our African ancestors were taken from their farms and villages and put in chains. They were forced onto a big ship and brought to America against their will. They were angry and afraid."

I close my eyes. I imagine the ship. My heart feels heavy as I see the faces of my ancestors.

The *Atlantic Slave Trade*, which lasted from the sixteenth to the nineteenth century, formed a triangle. First, European ships brought products to West Africa. The products were exchanged for people who were being held captive. The second leg, in which the captives were brought by force to the Americas, was the *Middle Passage*. On the third leg of the journey, the ships returned to Europe with raw materials received in exchange for the African captives.

Grandma continues, "The Africans would only eat the foods they knew from home: yams, rice, and—"

"Black-eyed peas?"

"Yes," Grandma says. "Black-eyed peas kept them alive. Now we eat them on New Year's Day for good luck."

Black-eyed peas are actually beans and are native to Africa. They can be cooked many ways and are a source of fiber, protein, copper, calcium, vitamin A, and iron. Since black-eyed peas swell when cooked, they have come to symbolize prosperity. Eating them on New Year's Day is said to bring wealth and happiness in the New Year.

Grandma rinses the black-eyed peas and puts them
in a pot to cook.

"Is it time to make pralines?" I ask eagerly.

"Not yet." Grandma takes a pan out of the
refrigerator. "It's time to check on my hoghead cheese."

I wrinkle my nose. I do not like hoghead cheese.
One, it's not really cheese. Two, it *really* is made
from a hog's head!

Yesterday, I peeked at the hog's head boiling in
Grandma's big pot. It was scary!

Grandma scraped
the meat off the bone,
mixed it with gelatin
and spices, and spread
it in a pan.

Pork: meat from a pig.
Hog: a domestic pig
that weighs more than
120 pounds.

Now I watch as she shakes the pan.
"Good!" she exclaims. "It's nice and firm."

"Grandma, why do you make hoghead cheese?"

"Well, after their terrible journey, our ancestors were brought here to Louisiana, where they were enslaved—forced to work without pay—on a big farm called a plantation. They picked cotton. They sowed rice. They cut sugarcane. Sunup to sundown."

Grandma cuts the hoghead cheese into squares. "Our ancestors were given a small amount of food, usually cornmeal, molasses, rice, and pork. They received the parts of the pig no one else wanted: the feet, tail, intestines, and head."

"Yuck."

"So," Grandma continues, "our ancestors made do with what they had. They stuffed bits of pork into the intestines to make the sausage we call andouille. They made many meals using rice: jambalaya, beans and rice, gumbo."

"Yum. I like rice!"

"They ate boiled pigs' feet. They cooked pig tails with greens. And," she adds with a little smile, "they made hoghead cheese." Grandma offers me a small piece.

I picture my great-great-great-grandmother making do. I take a bite. "Hmmm. Not too bad."

Early next morning, Grandma and I go to the garden
to pick turnip greens for our New Year's Day dinner.
We greet Grandpa, who is already there pulling weeds.
Grandpa shows me how to pull the turnips from the
ground by their leafy green stems.

"Did our ancestors who were slaves eat healthy foods, too?" I ask Grandma.

"Mais oui!" she replies. It sounds like "may we," but it means "oh yes."

"Our people have always planted gardens," Grandpa tells me.

"What did they grow in their gardens during slavery time?" I ask as I begin pulling turnips.

"They grew the same vegetables our ancestors grew in Africa," Grandpa answers, "and the same ones I grow in my garden today: beans and tomatoes, turnip greens and sweet potatoes."

"But when did they have time to tend their gardens?"

"Often on Saturdays, their workday ended at noon," Grandma explains. "So they had Saturday afternoon and Sunday to tend to their own needs."

Yams vs. Sweet Potatoes
Sweet potatoes have thin, smooth skin and usually have orange flesh.
Yams, which are native to Africa, tend to have tough skin and white flesh. In the United States, sweet potatoes are more common than yams. Both are packed with nutrients!

"They also went fishing in the Mississippi River. They caught crabs, shrimp, and oysters. Just like I did when I was a boy," recalls Grandpa. "That seafood made for some good gumbo!"

"They gathered pecans, too," Grandma adds. "They always had plenty of pecans and lots of sugar. That's why pralines are so popular."

"And because they're like a cookie and candy in one!" I chime in.

Grandma smiles. "So, by gardening, fishing, and gathering nuts and berries on their own time, our ancestors added variety to their diet."

Grandpa shakes his head in wonder. "And by sunup Monday, they were back in the fields."

"Looks like we have all the greens we need,
Frances," Grandma announces. "I'm going to
cook them with smoked turkey."

As Grandma and I head inside, Grandpa gives me a wink
and whispers, "Me, I still like my greens with pig tails."

In the kitchen, Grandma cuts the greens from the turnips. She stores the turnips for later, and I wash the greens. When they're nice and clean, Grandma puts them to boil on a back burner on the stove. "And now," she says like a TV announcer, "it is time to make . . ."

"Pralines!" I shout. "At last!"

"That's right!" Grandma says.

Once we've gathered the ingredients and utensils, Grandma heats the sugar and milk in a saucepan. She hands me the wooden spoon to stir while she checks her list.

"We need to make the gumbo. Your mom and aunties will bring the jambalaya and the rest."

THERMOMETER

WAX PAPER

WHITE SUGAR

BUTTER

BROWN SUGAR

"What a celebration it will be!" I exclaim as Grandma adds butter, then pecans, to the mixture. Something occurs to me as I stir: "Grandma, did our ancestors who were slaves ever have anything to celebrate?"

VANILLA

EVAPORATED

MILK

"Mais oui!" Grandma exclaims. "Even in the darkest days! Do you know what they celebrated?"

I think real hard. "Well, they had each other. And they had food to eat."

Grandma nods. "They set aside a part of their Sundays for worship, rest, and visiting. Families came together and, in good weather, cooked outside.

President Abraham Lincoln issued the Emancipation Proclamation on January 1, 1863, declaring that "all persons held as slaves" within the rebellious states "are, and henceforward shall be free." The 13th Amendment to the Constitution was passed by Congress on January 31, 1865, but not ratified by the states until December 6 of that year. Only then was slavery abolished in the entire United States.

"They celebrated the harvest, Christmas, and weddings. And they never gave up hope. One day, they were able to celebrate the most wonderful event of all."

"Freedom!" I shout.

"That's right. And by
that time, the foods they ate
had become a part of our
family tradition. These foods
remind us that we are here
and we are free because of
the hard work and sacrifices
of our ancestors."

"So, Grandma, we say
thank you to them by eating
the foods they ate—and by
making pralines!"

Grandma nods, smiling, as she
removes the saucepan from the burner.

After we add the vanilla, it's time for my favorite part of making pralines.

"Careful!" Grandma warns as she spreads butter onto wax paper. "It's very hot!"

I drop spoonfuls of the creamy mixture onto the wax paper.

I make sure there are big pieces of pecans in each spoonful.

Once they've cooled down, we each taste a praline. Delicious!

Finally it's New Year's Day!
My mom and dad, aunts,
uncles, and cousins arrive,
bringing more food.
There are hugs and kisses and
shouts of "Happy New Year!"

Grandma and Grandpa are beaming.
The house fills with laughter and
conversation as everyone shares news
and memories.

NEW YEAR'S DAY MENU

SEAFOOD GUMBO

JAMBALAYA

POTATO SALAD

BLACK-EYED PEAS

HOGHEAD CHEESE

TURNIP GREENS

RICE

RED BEANS WITH ANDOUILLE

SWEET POTATO PIE

PECAN PIE

PRALINES

After a while, we gather around the long dining room table and bow our heads in prayer.

Someone exclaims, "Bon appétit! Happy eating!" Then the feasting begins!

As we eat, I think about the story Grandma told me.
It was about our family and those who came before us.
About the foods we eat and why.
It made me sad, proud, and thankful. All at the same time!
That's why Grandma's kitchen is the best place to be.
There's always good food and lots of love.
And a story.

FAY'S FABULOUS PRALINES

Our mom taught my sister Faynessa how to make pralines.

INGREDIENTS AND UTENSILS

2 cups of pecan halves, toasted

1½ cup of white sugar

1½ cup of firmly packed brown sugar

1 can of evaporated milk

1 stick of butter

1 teaspoon of vanilla extract

Candy thermometer

Wooden spoon

Wax paper. Butter the paper! You'll see why.

DIRECTIONS

You will need the help of your grandma or any adult family member!

1. *Toast the pecans.* Spread them on a cookie sheet in one layer, and put them in a preheated oven at 350°F for ten minutes. Stay near the oven so they won't burn. Toasting the pecans makes them nice and crunchy.

2. *Pour the white and brown sugar and the milk into a heavy pot.* (Mom used a cast-iron pot.) Stir over medium heat for about ten minutes, until it turns into syrup. (Careful: Melted sugar is HOT.)

3. *Drop some syrup into a glass of cold water.* If it turns into threads of sugar, it's ready for the butter and pecans. Or test the mixture with a candy thermometer. The temperature should be at least 228°F.

4. *Add the butter and pecans.* And keep stirring! Drop some more syrup into cold water to see if it forms a soft candy ball, or use a candy thermometer to make sure the temperature is at least 236°F.

5. *Take the pot off the stove.* Add the vanilla, and stir with a wooden spoon for about two minutes, until the batter gets thick and turns a lighter color.

6. *Drop tablespoons full of batter* on the buttered wax paper—the butter keeps the pralines from sticking. The candy needs to cool off so you won't burn your hands or mouth. It will get smoother and harder and smell great.

And finally, you get to eat pralines you (and your helper) made with your own hands! Delicious? Yes. Cookie or candy? You be the judge! Bon appétit!

AUTHOR'S NOTE

Black-Eyed Peas and Hoghead Cheese: A Story of Food, Family, and Freedom traces the origins of African American foodways, or eating habits, from the point of view of one family preparing for a holiday dinner.

My inspiration was my own family and the celebrations we had when I was a little girl. I recalled the time I spent in both my mother's kitchen in Los Angeles and my grandmother's kitchen in Vacherie, Louisiana. My family has deep roots in Louisiana, which is why *Black-Eyed Peas and Hoghead Cheese* has a definite Creole flavor.

The term "Creole" can mean many things. It is the name of the language my mother grew up speaking, but it also refers to people and a way of cooking. In Louisiana, the language, the food, and the culture evolved from the interactions of people with West African, French, Spanish, and Indigenous backgrounds.

In my family, celebrations always began in the kitchen. I remember my grandmother's big kitchen being more like a family room. (Somehow, though, when I visited as an adult, the kitchen had shrunk.) I can still see my grandfather's rocking chair in the corner.

The kitchen was where stories were told. As we children listened to the stories of our elders, we gained a sense of pride, identity, and belonging. We felt love. That's what I remember the most: the feelings I experienced when we were preparing for a holiday. The aromas, the laughter, the singing. As a skinny kid, I did not have a big appetite, but, oh, how I ate up the stories. Our stories, foods, and traditions are inseparable from our history. Not keeping them would be like taking the rice out of jambalaya!

Black-Eyed Peas and Hoghead Cheese is one small contribution to the tragic, stirring, triumphant history of soul food and the resilient, brave, resourceful people who created it. There are many foodways. Sharing our traditions with others is a way of bringing people together. Perhaps the foods your family members eat and the stories they tell represent another part of African or African American culture. Or your family's stories and foodways might come from an entirely different part of the world.

All of our stories are important.

And the best ones begin in the kitchen.

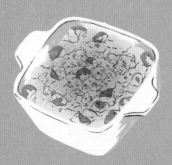
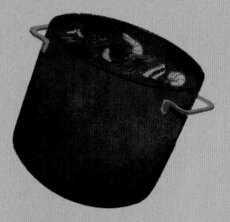

SOURCES

Bower, Anne L., ed. *African American Foodways: Explorations of History & Culture*. Chicago: University of Illinois Press, 2007.

Covey, Herbert C., and Dwight Eisnach. *What the Slaves Ate: Recollections of African American Foods and Foodways from the Slave Narratives*. Santa Barbara, CA: Greenwood Press, 2009.

Harris, Jessica B. *High on the Hog: A Culinary Journey from Africa to America*. New York: Bloomsbury, 2011.

Miller, Adrian. *Soul Food: The Surprising Story of an American Cuisine, One Plate at a Time*. Chapel Hill: The University of North Carolina Press, 2013.

FURTHER READING

Archer, Joe, and Caroline Craig. *Plant, Cook, Eat! A Children's Cookbook*. Watertown, MA: Charlesbridge, 2018.

Hall, Carla, with Genevieve Ko. *Carla Hall's Soul Food: Everyday and Celebration*. New York: Harper Wave, 2018.

Johnson, JJ, and Alexander Smalls, with Veronica Chambers. *Between Harlem and Heaven: Afro-Asian-American Cooking for Big Nights, Weeknights, and Every Day*. New York: Flatiron Books, 2018.

Samuelsson, Marcus, with Osayi Endolyn, Yewande Komolafe, and Tamie Cook. *The Rise: Black Cooks and the Soul of American Food*. New York: Voracious, 2020.

My mom's pot for gumbo and hoghead cheese is over sixty-five years old.